HARUTAKA NAKAWATARI

The Sea and I

Translated by Susan Matsui

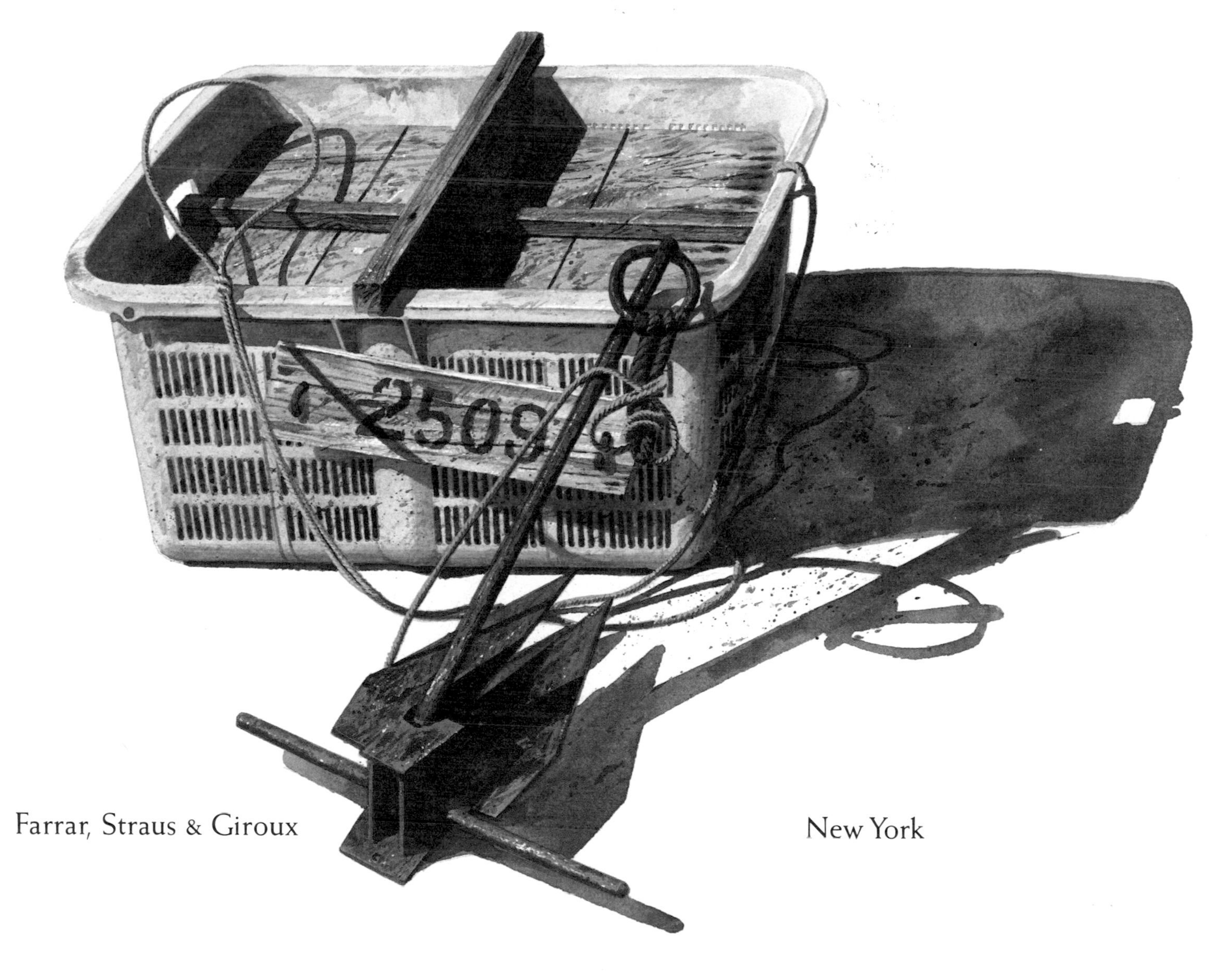

Farrar, Straus & Giroux New York

From almost anywhere on our island, you can hear the sound of the waves lapping the beach.

Every day, my father goes fishing.

At dawn, I go with him to the shore and watch his boat leave.

Today the breeze is so strong that I can hear waves crashing on the beach.

A flock of gulls
is flying into the
harbor. Do they
know if a storm
is coming?

Z61 3725
良
白

Clouds surge across the sky as I run along the breakwater.

The waves are rough and threatening.
"Hey, sea gull, is my father's boat safe?"

The gull flies away.

I follow the bird down the beach.
Waves thunder at the foot of the cliff.

There's the lighthouse!
A fierce wind buffets the headland.

I brace myself to keep from being blown away. The sea gull and I watch the horizon. We do not see Father's boat. Is he all right?

Evening comes, and at last the sea grows calm. As I walk down to the harbor, the water is sparkling like silver. A boat is coming in.

Father waves as he always does, to let me know he is home safe.

I wave, to let him know I have been watching for him.

With a warm smile, he gives me a big sea hug.

Father loves the sea, and I love him.

I listen to the many stories Father tells of his voyages.

The sound of the waves carries my dreams far, far away.

Library of Congress catalog card number: 91-34364
Originally published in Japan under the title *Umi-to Boku*
by Fukutake Publishing Co., Ltd., 1990
Published simultaneously in Canada by HarperCollins*CanadaLtd*
Printed and bound in the United States of America
by Horowitz/Rae Book Manufacturers
First American edition, 1992